HOLLY KELLER

Geraldine First

Greenwillow Books, New York

For Corey
and Jesse

Watercolor paints and a black pen were
used for the full-color art. The text type is
Geometric 706 Medium.

Printed in Singapore by Tien Wah Press
First Edition 10 9 8 7 6 5 4 3 2 1

Library of Congress
Cataloging-in-Publication Data
Keller, Holly.
Geraldine first / by Holly Keller.
      p.   cm.
Summary: Geraldine the pig hates to have
her little brother Willie copy her behavior
and finally discovers one activity which he
won't imitate.
ISBN 0-688-14149-8 (trade).
ISBN 0-688-14150-1 (lib. bdg.)
[1. Pigs—Fiction.   2. Brothers and
sisters—Fiction.   3. Family life—Fiction.
4. Behavior—Fiction.] I. Title.
PZ7.K28132Gac   1996   [E]—dc20
95-2258   CIP   AC

"Bath time, Geraldine," Mama called.

"Willie first," Geraldine called back.
"I'm always first," Willie cried.
"Not true," Geraldine shouted.

"Don't shout, Geraldine," Papa scolded.
"We'll have dinner first," Mama said,
   and she sighed.

"Ugh," said Geraldine when she came into the kitchen.
"No beans."

"Beans make you strong," Papa said.

"I'm strong now," Geraldine insisted, and she picked up
 Willie and plopped him into his chair.

"No beans," Willie said, and he giggled.
"Don't copy me," Geraldine said.

"Carrots are bad too," she grumbled,
  and she took them off her plate.
"Carrots are good for your eyes," said Papa,
  and he put them back.
"Maybe if I don't eat them, I won't see Willie,"
  Geraldine argued, and she made a face.

Willie made a face too.
"Stop copying me, Willie," Geraldine snapped.

Geraldine drank her milk and held up the glass
to look through the bottom.
"I can see you," she said to Papa.
Willie held up his glass too.
"I can see you, Geraldine," he said.

Geraldine put down her glass with a thud.
"I said don't copy me, Willie!"
"That's enough, Geraldine," Mama said sternly.

Geraldine didn't want any dessert,
so she went to play in her room.

Willie came in later to see what she was doing.
Geraldine was building a tower with her blocks.
Willie built one too.

"Uh-ohhhh," he cried when his tower toppled
onto Geraldine's.
"I'm sure he didn't mean it," Mama told Geraldine.
"I'll help you make another one," Papa offered.

"NO," Geraldine said angrily.
"NO," Willie echoed.
 Geraldine gnashed her teeth.
"Willie, WILL YOU PLEASE STOP COPYING ME!"
"Put away your toys now, Geraldine," Mama said.
"It's getting late."

In a few minutes Willie heard Geraldine banging around
in her room. He peeked in the door.
"What are you doing, Geraldine?" he whispered.
"Cleaning," Geraldine mumbled,
and she picked up some blocks.

Willie picked up a block too, and Geraldine groaned.
Then she smiled. . . .
"Willie," she said, "I have to clean my room.
Don't get in my way."

She picked up a few more blocks and waited.

"Now I'll put away the doll's clothes," she announced loudly.

Geraldine picked up a book and a few crayons.

But when she started to put away the tea set,
Willie didn't budge.
"I'm tired," he said, and he left.
Geraldine laughed. Then she went to find Mama.

"I'm ready for my bath now," she said.
"Willie is tired, so I'll be first."
"Geraldine is first!" Mama proclaimed.
"And first is just fine with me.
 How about some bubble bath?"
 Geraldine nodded happily,
 and Mama took her upstairs.